STECK-VAUGHN

PAIR-IT BOOKS™

The Neighborhood Party

Written by Katherine Mead
Illustrated by Tom Barrett

STECK-VAUGHN ®
COMPANY
ELEMENTARY • SECONDARY • ADULT • LIBRARY

We had a surprise party.
Dan brought the hats.

2

We had a surprise party.
Maria brought the cake.

3

We had a surprise party.
Lee brought the candles.

4

We had a surprise party.
Kate brought the ice cream.

We had a surprise party.
James brought the bowls.

We had a surprise party.
Nick just brought his pet.

We had a surprise!